CONTENTS

CHAPTER 1

Ribena on the Rocks

Bertie picked up his glass and looked at the playing cards in his hand. He swirled the drink round. The ice clinking together was the only sound in the room before he took a gulp and held the glass up to his head so that the ice from his favourite cocktail would cool his thoughts.

Bertie scanned the room. It was dark and thick layers of cigar smoke twisted in mid-air, churned out by fellow members of the Empire Club. This was the place where great men with too much time on their hands and too much money in their bank accounts hung out. They talked about the good old days as they dreamed up new and interesting ways to take money off each other.

"Another Ribena on the rocks with a twist. In fact, make it a double," Bertie said, and handed his glass to a waiter. Bertie scanned his cards again and looked at the table, where a pile of money sat just begging to be won at the end of another tense game of cards.

"Oh, do hurry up, Bertie," one of the other players said. "Some of us have dinner plans, you know!"

"Don't listen to him, Bertie, you keep playing!" Ginger snapped. He was the third player at the table and Bertie's oldest school pal. "I've got my eye on a Bentley, and your winnings would come in handy."

Bertie's nickname was "Unlucky". "Unlucky Bertie" everyone called him at the Empire Club, because of his amazing losing streak. Not once in all his 57 years on the planet had Bertie ever won anything. Not a game of rugby, not a game of I spy, KerPlunk, polo, badminton – not a bean. And every time he lost, there was always a cry of, "Oh, unlucky, Bertie …!" So that's how his nickname began.

You might think that someone who lost as often in life as Bertie wouldn't have any friends, or any money for that matter. But there was one thing that Bertie had going for him: he was a blue-blooded royal – Prince Bertrand Montgomery, Duke of Scotland, to give him his full name. And his older sister – well, she was the queen of England.

Yes, that's right, even in the great game of life Bertie had come second. While his sister got to wear a crown and have people bow to her, Bertie had to make do with spending his time losing at cards and trying to stay out of trouble. So far it wasn't going well.

But maybe, just maybe, Bertie's luck was about to change.

He looked at his cards once again.

"OK, OK, I'll bet the lot!" Bertie said. Suddenly he just knew he had to win. Surely, *surely*, this time his luck would change. "I'll go all in!"

There were gasps from everyone around him.

"HOW ALL IN?" Ginger barked back.

"I'll throw in the Rolls-Royce!" Bertie said, frisbee-ing the keys across the table.

"I'll bet my country mansion!" Ginger said, getting caught up in it all.

"Which one?"

"The one in France!" Ginger grinned.

"I'll bet half of Scotland!" Bertie grinned back.

"Which half?"

"The top half," Bertie blurted out.

"I'll bet all I have!" Ginger said. "The houses, the bank accounts, the business, my seat at the cricket – EVERYTHING!"

"I'll bet my lot too!" Bertie said gleefully. "The jewels, the palaces, the crowns, the titles. If you win, you can have everything. You can be the king of England!" Bertie got out a notepad and wrote "IOU – everything!" on it.

The gasps got louder. Bertie looked at his cards again. All he needed was the right card from the pack to have the perfect hand.

He'd been watching the cards all game and he was pretty sure he knew where every single one was. There was one card left – face down on the table. Bertie knew it was the one he needed. He took a deep breath and went for it; it was all or nothing, now or never!

He smiled a winning smile before picking it up from the table. "Master Plod, the policeman's son!" he said, throwing it down with the rest of his cards. "Happy Families!" he bellowed before downing his drink in one. "I'm not so—"

"Unlucky, Bertie!" everyone in the club cried out.

"What?!" Bertie said, looking down at his cards. A stupid smile grinned back at him from Mr Bun, the baker, and not Master Plod. "No, it can't be. Where's Master Plod?" he said, beginning to panic. What had he just done?

"I've got it!" Ginger smiled, showing it to Bertie. "That, dear old chap, is Happy Families. That makes you the loser and me – what was it again?" he said, looking at Bertie's IOU. "Oh yes,

king of England, and I still have enough for a
Bentley!" he said, scooping the rest of the cash.

"Oh, Bertie, what have you done?" came
the cries from the other club members, and
that was the last thing Bertie heard before
everything went black.

CHAPTER 2

Out-of-Touch Oiks

Bertie rubbed his head and opened his eyes. "Oh my, what a terrible dream," he said.

His sister, the Queen, was standing next to him. "Agh! Hello, Betty, dear," Bertie groaned. "Oh, I had such a nightmare. Is it time for breakfast? Can I have a dippy egg?" He smiled.

The Queen looked at him for a long time before she lifted her queenly handbag into the air. There was a loud thud of leather against head and everything went black again.

"Oh my, what a terrible dream within a dream," Bertie said as he woke up for the second time. "Can I have a dippy egg … wait, haven't we done this already, sis?"

"Get up!" the Queen barked.

Bertie jumped to his feet, rubbed his eyes and looked around. He wasn't in his bedroom after all. He was in the Empire Club surrounded by his pals, and that meant … "Oh no, it wasn't a dream?" he asked.

The Queen shook her head.

"Doesn't that mean …?" he said, looking at the table of cards and money.

"YES!" the Queen said. "I knew something awful had happened when they rang me; they only ever ring me when it's bad news, Bertie." The Queen pushed a piece of paper at him. "It's a strange thing, the law. Did you know that if you write an IOU note and sign it, it counts as a

contract, AND THERE'S NOTHING YOU CAN DO
ABOUT IT?!"

"You mean we've lost everything?" Bertie
said, beginning to whimper.

"NO, BERTIE, IT MEANS *YOU'VE* LOST
EVERYTHING!" the Queen snapped, and swung

her bag at Bertie again. This time Bertie ducked.

"But you're the queen, can't you just throw Ginger in the Tower? No offence, Ginger ..." Bertie said, looking over at his old mate, who was busy trying on an upside-down lampshade as a crown. "Or, you know, chop his head off a bit?"

"NO! I am the head of state, not a children's book character. You can't go around murdering people who annoy you. If I could, I'd have turned you into sausages years ago, Bertie. We are finished! There is only one thing to try to do, one person who can save us ..." The Queen sighed.

"BATMAN?" Bertie asked.

"The Prime Minister, Bertie. PREPARE MY CARRIAGE! WE'RE OFF TO DOWNING STREET!"

*

"Hello, Your Majesty. What can I do for you? I am your humble servant," the Prime Minister said, bowing. "This makes a change; normally I come to your place." The Prime Minister grinned.

"Hello, Prime Minister. As you know, we've always been good friends ..." the Queen started.

Bertie stood next to her, head down, bow tie undone, cheeks red with shame. Behind her stood drivers and footmen, ladies-in-waiting, trumpeters and other servants. The Queen never travelled anywhere on her own, whether she was nipping to the loo or dragging her useless brother from the Empire Club to Downing Street, home of Bob Bobswell, the Prime Minister.

"Good friends, are we?" the Prime Minister said, looking a bit surprised. "The first time we met, you called me an oik."

"I meant it in a good way – who doesn't love an oik?!" The Queen laughed nervously. "Listen, Prime Minister, may I call you Bob? I'll cut to the chase. We need your help. Bertie here," the Queen said, pointing at her brother, who looked up to do a little wave, "well, he's rather put us on a sticky wicket by flushing all the Montgomery marmalade down the pan in a moment of monkey play."

"Translator!" the Prime Minister yelled.

"He lost all the wonga on a game of cards," the Prime Minister's assistant whispered into his ear.

"Oh," the Prime Minister replied.

"Now, I've had a word with Ginger, the person who won the game of cards ..."

"Hello!" Ginger waved from the back of the crowd.

"Yes, anyway ..." the Queen carried on. "I think we can pay off Ginger with a stack of cash so we can remain royal. All we need is 20 or 30 million pounds, and he'll be fine and it'll be the end of it. Isn't that right, Ginger?"

"Err ..."

"30 million?!" the Prime Minister said. "Where are you going to get that?"

"You're going to give it to me!" The Queen smiled.

"No, I'm not," the Prime Minister said, shaking his head.

"But I'm the queen, the public love me and my family ... you can't get rid of us. You can't put Ginger in charge!" the Queen gasped.

"The public don't love you. Have you seen the newspapers?" the Prime Minister said. He picked up a few papers to show her. "This is the latest in a long line of royal disasters."

The Prime Minister shook his head. "There was that time you burned your castle down, Your Majesty, because it was raining and someone thought it would be a laugh to have a fireworks party indoors. We paid for that to be rebuilt. Plus there was the royal yacht. Remember when you all went skinny dipping and forgot to drop the anchor and the yacht floated away? That was your son Harry's fault, wasn't it? We still haven't found that thing, so you made us build you a new one, to your design ... the one that sank when it was launched. I mean, who puts windows on the bottom of a yacht!"

"Sorry," Bertie said. "I wanted to watch the fishies swim by."

"Everything you lot do is a disaster and, no, I'm afraid, Your Majesty, the public don't like you, truth be told. We all think you're a bunch of spoilt, out-of-touch oiks!" the Prime Minister yelled. "Ginger!"

"Yes, sir," Ginger replied.

"Do you want the job? Being king of England?" the Prime Minister asked.

"Erm, OK," Ginger said.

"Well, it's yours. You won it fair and square. I declare you king," the Prime Minister said, and waved his hand around. He pointed at all the Queen's servants. "Ginger, I think all these people in wigs and fancy frocks belong to you now. Your Former Majesty, I'm afraid you lot are on your own."

CHAPTER 3

A Palace or a Pint of Milk?

"YOUR BROTHER IS AN IDIOT, BETTY! WHY DON'T WE JUST DO THE SENSIBLE THING AND THROW HIM TO THE DOGS?! No offence, Bertie," George yelled. Prince George was the Queen's husband, an old army man. He was a no-nonsense type who said what he liked, when he liked.

"HE HAS NO BRAIN. ALL THAT'S INSIDE HIS HEAD IS JELLY. HE'S THE MOST USELESS HUMAN I'VE EVER MET! AGAIN, NO OFFENCE!"

"No, well, it's a fair point," Bertie muttered with a shrug.

"I agree, George, but what else can we do? We have no home, we are basically not royal any more, you're no longer a prince and neither is he!" the Ex-Queen said, pointing at Bertie. "And I'm no longer the flipping Queen. We have nothing. We have no servants, we have nowhere to live and we have to move out tomorrow! Now, I suggest we each pick a wing of the palace and look for whatever loose change we can find. Look down the back of all the sofas, look underneath beds and meet back here in an hour. We can then pool the cash to see what we can come up with to buy us a new house!"

"Right, good plan, dear!" George agreed. "Let's go!" he said, with a salute to no one in particular. And with that, all three of them walked off in different directions towards different parts of the palace.

"OW!" they all cried out together as they each banged into a closed door.

"There's no one to open them any more, is there?" George said, rubbing his head. "Well, I used to open doors in the army way back when. I suppose I can do it again. It never leaves, you know, the training."

He smirked, and with that he grabbed the door handle. "Now watch me. You grab it here and give it a pull, like so," he said, showing his wife and brother-in-law how doors work.

"After three!" he said, and on three they all grabbed and pulled. "You see, we're free! Right, see you back here in a bit!"

*

Bertie had been looking round his bedroom for a while and had collected quite a haul of loot. There was a bag of it, mostly foreign dosh left over from his many holidays, and a few medals that his great-grandfather Albert had won for invading a far-off place a very long time ago.

He also had a painting that hung on his wall; he had no idea if it was worth anything, but it was old and French and those guys were really good at art, so it was bound to help in some way.

"Bertie, Bertie!" The door swung open and Bertie's wife, Margo, marched in.

"Hey, how did you do that? I didn't know you were in the army!" Bertie said. He'd never seen his wife opening a door before, and he had to admit she was pretty good at it.

"Bertie, is it true? I heard it on the news. Are we … poor?!" she squealed.

"Yes, dear, I'm sorry. In some ways I blame myself!" Bertie said.

"Why, Bertie dear? What happened?"

"Well, because I sort of lost everything playing with the Empire lot again."

"EVERYTHING?"

"Everything." Bertie nodded.

"EVERYTHING?"

"EVERYTHING."

"EVERYTHING?!"

"EVERYTHING." Bertie nodded.

"Well, what are we doing about it?" Margo wailed.

"How much is that necklace worth?" Bertie said, looking at her jewellery.

*

"£177,842.27 and a bag of old buttons," the
Ex-Queen said, looking at the pile on the table.

"OK, is that a lot of money?" Margo said.
"I mean, I don't really know how money works.
Will this buy us a palace or a pint of milk?"

"Hmm, good question. I don't really use money either. Who do we know that uses money?" the Ex-Queen asked.

"I use it!" Bertie said.

"No, you *lose* it," George said.

"Well, I know how we can find out what it will buy us. Look, I have an app," explained Bertie. "It's called Right Movers. You can find houses on there. I looked at it when we wanted a new palace, except they don't really sell palaces on there. Anyway, let's have a look. I can enter the amount of money in this box here. Then we need a location …"

"How about Windsor?" the Ex-Queen said.

Bertie typed it in and tapped search. "And there we are!" he said.

A list of houses popped up. Bertie, the Ex-Queen, George and Margo all leaned in.

"They're a bit … small …" Margo said, squinting at the screen.

"Oh no, these are just photos. They'll be normal house size in real life." Bertie smiled.

"I think what Margo means is that the *houses* are small. This one only has three bedrooms," the Ex-Queen said.

"Which one?" Bertie said.

"That one, on King Street." George pointed it out.

"Oh, this one?" Bertie said, pointing at the screen.

"NO!" everyone yelled as Bertie's finger hit the screen.

"Congratulations on your purchase. Your offer has been accepted!" the phone said.

"Bertie!" Margo yelled. "You just bought a flipping house! Near Windsor!"

"Why Windsor?" George asked.

"Hey, your wife chose the location," Bertie said.

"Why Windsor?" Margo asked.

"Because," the Ex-Queen said, "it's near Eton. It's near Harry's school, or his old school. We can't afford to send him there any more."

"Oh, I forgot about Harry ..." Bertie said with a sigh.

CHAPTER 4

King Street

"I'm sorry, what now, Mr Beans?" Harry said, looking straight at the headmaster. "You want me to leave? You can't ask me to leave. I am Prince Harry, future King of England and the other bits ..."

"Yes, well, you'll have to get used to being just plain old Harry. You're going to another school now," the headmaster said.

"I'm moving schools? Is there some sort of transfer for school children that I didn't know about? Oh, I hope I'm not off to Harrow, I heard it's an absolute dive. They only have one lacrosse pitch, ONE. I mean, talk about slumming it."

"No, you're not going there. Have you heard of St Grimley's Comprehensive?" the headmaster asked politely.

"What's a comprehensive?" Harry asked.

"Well, you'll find out. Oh, I need you to hand in your top hat and pocket watch," Mr Beans said, as if Harry was a dirty cop handing back his badge and shooter.

"I'm going now?" Harry asked. "Is the car waiting outside?"

"Nope. Have you heard of something called a bus?"

"Of course I've heard of a bus. I even saw one once in a book." Harry smiled.

"Good, because yours leaves in about ten minutes. It's the number 21 and it takes you to King Street in Windsor – or almost!" Mr Beans said, pointing at the door.

*

"So here we are," the Ex-Queen said, looking at her new home. It was a tiny house crammed in among other tiny houses. The Ex-Queen could see curtains twitch in the houses next door as her new neighbours looked out to see what was going on.

"How are you feeling, Your Former Majesty?" a TV reporter asked. The whole world had heard about the move, and everyone wanted to know more.

"All right, let's step back and give these people some space," a policeman said, moving the press away. "You've got your pictures, now let them be."

"Hello! I'm Winnie," a woman said, walking up to the Ex-Queen and holding out her hand.

The Ex-Queen stared back. "Oh, my dear, you're supposed to curtsey."

"Errr," Winnie said, bending her knees and bobbing her head.

"Yes, everyone knows that!" George said as he, Margo and Bertie looked at their new home. Margo was on her horse, Blossom.

"Excuse me," Margo said, turning to Winnie, "where does one normally park one's horse?"

"What?"

"Ignore her, Winnie. Tell me, what do you do?" the Ex-Queen asked.

"I run the local neighbourhood watch group. Welcome to the street," said Winnie, and handed the Ex-Queen a fruit basket.

"How fascinating. Now, if you could bring our things inside, that would be super!"

"I'm not here to unpack for you!" Winnie snapped.

"Well, who is?" the Ex-Queen asked. "You can't expect us to do it!"

"What they say about you in the papers is right," Winnie huffed. "I'm off, and I'm taking my kiwis with me," she said, and grabbed the basket of fruit back.

"No, wait! Please can we have this kind gift back?" the Ex-Queen said. "We don't have any money!"

"Fine, have it, but you might want to try not being rude. And if you want to earn some money, you'd better start thinking about getting a job," Winnie said. "Like we all have to do here in the real world."

"Get a job?!" said the Ex-Queen, sounding shocked. It wasn't something she'd ever had to think about before. She knew at once that Winnie was right, but what on earth was she going to do?

"Oh, maybe I could be a lion tamer?" Bertie said, joining them.

"You're allergic to cats." Margo sighed.

"You need to find something a bit more suited to your skills. I was a dinner lady for 25 years," Winnie said proudly. "Give me a couple of spuds and a tin of beans and I can feed a school!"

"But we don't have any skills!" the Ex-Queen, Bertie, Margo and George said at once.

"Everyone's got skills," Winnie told them. "You just need to work out what they are. But I best go just now. My Bill will be home soon and he'll be after his tea. Keep the fruit basket and remember manners cost nothing," Winnie said. "And just to show there's no hard feelings, I'll pop back in a minute with some potatoes and beans."

The Ex-Queen took a deep breath and a good look at her new home. This was it: no more palaces, no more garden parties, no more untold riches. This was their new life. Her name had better change too. "From now on, I want you all to call me Betty. I am not the Queen any more. I think the sooner we get used to it the better," Betty announced.

*

Within a few hours all the royals, or rather ex-royals, were unpacked and trying to get used to their new lives in King Street.

"Sis ..." Bertie said, stumbling out of his new bedroom.

"ARGH!" Betty shouted. "You look like a ghost!!" Bertie stood in front of her with a sheet thing over his head.

"I was trying to make my bed. I was putting the duvet in the cover when I got lost. Can you help me out?"

"You're stuck in a duvet cover!" Betty said with a shake of her head.

"I panicked and took a wrong turning. Now I can't get out," Bertie said sadly.

"Look, Betty, I found a hat!" Margo said, walking in with a colander on her head.

Suddenly there was a HUGE bang from downstairs.

"WHAT WAS THAT?!" Betty yelled to George. "ALL I ASKED WAS FOR YOU TO OPEN A COUPLE OF TINS OF BEANS!"

"I couldn't find the tin opener, so I shot the lids off!" George yelled back.

"Those beans from Winnie were our dinner. Now we're going to starve!"

"Relax, sis," Bertie said. "I have an app on my phone. We can get pizza. It's like really round cheese on toast."

"Good. Let's hope they accept tiaras as payment." Betty sighed.

*

"KNOCK, KNOCK!" came the thump at the door.

"Hello, the pizza's here!" Margo said. "This is exciting: ordering pizza, it arriving. It's just like in the movies."

"KNOCK, KNOCK, KNOCK, KNOCK!"

"All right, all right!" Margo yelled, rushing to the door. "I hope you remembered my spicy wings! Oh, Harry!" she said, answering the door. "Everyone, it's Harry. Bravo, Harry, for getting a job and bringing us our pizza. Where is it?"

"I am not a pizza boy!" he snapped, standing on the front doorstep. "Can someone tell me what's going on? I have just caught a bus. Do you know how one catches a bus? One has to wait for ages at the bus stop. Then you get on, they drive you somewhere near your house and you get out again. One has to walk and do map reading," Harry said. "All I had was this address. I had to ask a perfect stranger where I live. Why don't I live where I live any more? Why am I going to a new school and why do you all think I'm a pizza delivery boy?!"

"PIZZA!" the real pizza boy said, walking up behind Harry at the front door.

"Be a good lad and pay the pizza boy, Harry, and we'll fill you in," Betty said.

Half an hour later the pizza was gone, as well as all Harry's hopes that this was a big mix-up.

"So I have to go to a new school because of this ... this ... NINCOMPOOP!" Harry yelled at Bertie.

"LANGUAGE, HARRY!" Betty yelled. "Bertie is my brother, your uncle. We are family and that means pretending to like each other."

"Thanks, dear sis," Bertie smiled. "I think that this may actually bring us all together in some strange way."

"Yeah, don't push it, idiot boy," Betty snapped. "Remember it's your fault that we're in this mess. The fact is, we need ... jobs," Betty said.

There were gasps from around the table.

"We need to learn to work!"

Again, there were huge gasps.

"This is our new life now. That includes you, Harry. No more expensive schools. We need to learn to be ... normal!"

CHAPTER 5

Not Right for Work

A couple of days later, Margo flounced into the kitchen. "It's no good, I'm just not right for work!" she wailed. "Nobody will give me a job!"

"What jobs have you gone for?" Betty asked.

"Well, as you know, I've always liked travelling," Margo said. "So I thought I'd try a job where you can travel around, but can you believe it takes years of training to be able to fly a plane? Then I thought about something in fashion, so I went to that department store in town to help people dress better, a bit like a stylist. You know, saying, 'Don't wear that, change your hair, that make-up isn't your colour, dear.' That sort of thing."

"That sounds perfect," Betty said. "What went wrong? Didn't you get on with your boss? Ooh … look what I can do. I found a video on the YouTube showing me how to make a perfect cup of tea!" She smiled.

"Boss? Oh no, it wasn't a job," said Margo. "I thought I'd just give it a go, you know, like training for a job if it ever came up, but the shop just called security and I had to leave."

"HA HA!" Bertie laughed.

"Well, that's not very nice, Bertie," Margo said.

"Oh no, I wasn't laughing at you, dear. There's a funny person on the internet doing funny things with his cat. He does make me chuckle."

"Let's have a look," Margo said as she grabbed the phone. "Goodness me, is that how many followers that person has? Nearly 12 million for larking about with a kitten."

"Yes, well, that's what he does," Bertie said.

"Bertie, can I borrow your phone?" Margo asked, and sat down at the kitchen table.

"Morning, Mumsie," Harry said, coming into the kitchen. "I'm ready to go."

"First day of school, exciting times!" George said, tucking into his egg and mini army of toast soldiers.

"Now, Harry, it's very important that you make an effort to fit in. You need to try to get on with the other boys and girls," Betty said.

"Girls?! They have girls at this school?" Harry said. He grinned. "Maybe this won't be so bad after all."

"Harry!" Betty said. "You need to focus on your studies!"

"Oh, OK. Don't worry, Mumsie. I'll work hard and do my best to fit in," Harry said. He grabbed his fencing swords. "Toddle pip," he said, walking to the front door. "Did you see where I put my oars?"

"In the hall, dear," Betty said.

"Byeeeee!" Harry said. "Oh, Mumsie, there's a man here to see you."

"Hello, excuse me …?" a man said, stepping into the kitchen.

"Yes?" Betty said.

"I'm Bill. Is that your horse outside? What am I saying? Of course it is. Can you at least tie him up? I'm your neighbour from next door, you see …"

"It's a her!" Margo snorted, looking up from Bertie's phone. "And no, I won't. Blossom doesn't like being tied up."

"Well, she's doing her business all over my garden!" the man said.

"Oh gosh, there are so many rules to follow on this street. FINE!" Margo sighed. She handed Bertie his phone and headed outside.

"Shame, really," Bill said. "We could have done with that sort of deposit at the allotment." He sighed.

"Deposit?" George asked.

"Manure from the horse, it's very good for the vegetables. It's just what we need. Oh, I'm a member of the Allotment Association. Bill's the name, growing stuff's my game," Bill said, and he showed George his badge.

"That looks like a medal," George said.

"Well, we run a tight ship. I like to think of our little gang as my soldiers."

"Well, sign me up. Lord Lieutenant George Montgomery reporting for duty, SIR!" George shouted with a salute.

"Crikey. OK," Bill said. "I wasn't expecting that. I'd best show you where we keep the spades."

"INFLUENCER!" Margo suddenly yelled, coming back into the house and bringing the horse with her.

"Who's got influenza?" asked Betty.

"No, not influenza – influencer. I'm going to be an influencer," Margo said. "All I need is a phone. Oh, can I borrow your phone again, Bertie?"

Bertie nodded.

"Great. I'm going to be an internet person who is famous for being on the internet and speaking and things," Margo said.

"Why don't you get a proper job?" Betty said.

"This is a proper job! You can make loads of money from it. All you need is lots of time to waste on the phone and you don't have to worry about anyone else."

"Then you're perfect, dear." Betty smiled. "What about you, Bertie, what's your job? Margo has her internet thingy, George is going to grow things, Harry's off to school. What about you?"

"Well ..." Bertie started. "I thought I might go and have a bath."

"Oh, Bertie." His sister sighed.

"Well, what about you?" Bertie asked.

"I'm sure something will turn up ..." Betty said hopefully.

Just at that second there was another knock on the door.

CHAPTER 6

Welcome to Showbiz

"Hello?" Betty said, opening the door slowly.

"Hello!" someone answered in a jolly voice.

"Who are you?"

"Herbert Plug," the man said, lifting his hat off his head.

"No, really, what's your name?"

"Herbert Plug, from Plug and Sons, agents to the stars. We take dreams and put them on the silver screen!" he said with a big smile.

"Agents?"

"Oh yes, we represent some of the biggest, best stars in film and on telly. You know that bloke from the insurance ad who sings that song? There's him … and a couple of others."

"Oh. Sorry, why are you here?" Betty asked.

"I'll tell you why, your Ex-Maj. Let's talk the future. There is quite a bit of money to be made from being on the TV, for someone like you."

"Someone like me?"

"Yes, now don't take this the wrong way, but you were huge. I mean, the queen is about as big as it gets. Palaces, crowns and, now, well, you've ended up here," Herbert said as he walked into the house. "It's a fall from grace, it's a story of having it all and now having nothing!"

"Goodness me," Betty said, not used to people speaking to her so bluntly.

"Three words, *Celebrity Love Island*," Herbert said. "*Strictly Come Dancing. I'm a Celebrity.* I can get you work; I can get you good money."

"Good money?"

"Big money!" Herbert said.

"Big money?" Betty muttered. "How much, you know, to be on a television show? You know, the dancing one, the one I've actually seen?"

"Thousands," Herbert said. "That would be for one of the big shows, like *Strictly*, and that's where we can end up – but we need to start small. I've got a supermarket that needs someone to cut a big ribbon with a pair of giant scissors right now. They're waiting on the phone. What do you say, Your Ex-Maj? 500 quid, cash in hand, minus 45% for me."

"OK," Betty said.

"Brilliant. Welcome to showbiz, you're going to love it!"

*

"Hello? Margo?" Bertie called out as he came downstairs again after his morning bath. "Hello, where is everyone? Hello? I don't like being all alone. I get scared and also a bit bored."

Bertie picked up a note from Margo on the kitchen table. It said: "Gone out influencing".

"Sis?" Bertie called out. Nothing. "George is off doing gardening things. I need to do something," Bertie said to himself. "You know, show I'm doing my bit. I know, I could cook something? What's their favourite? Oh yes, a nice roast swan. Now, where do you find a swan …? THE FRIDGE!"

Bertie walked over to the fridge. There were a few bits and bobs that Betty had grabbed from the cook's kitchen in the palace before they left, but sadly a swan wasn't one of them.

"Hmm, OK, so no swan. Wait a second, what's that?!"

A big juicy, plump pigeon had just landed on the garden fence.

"Perfect!" Bertie said, and grabbed his old butterfly net from the box in the corner.

CHAPTER 7

Pigeon Fancier

Bertie crouched at one side of the window and kept his eye on the pigeon. He took a deep breath before doing a commando roll to the other side of the window, only to get tangled in the curtains. Luckily he was able to karate chop himself out of trouble.

"Take that, you big curtain assassin!" Bertie yelled. The pigeon hadn't even noticed Bertie yet. "Once you're cooked, no one will know you're not a swan," Bertie muttered. "I mean, yes, you might be a bit smaller, but I'll just tell them you shrank in the oven."

Next, Bertie opened the back door like a ninja – a ninja in a bath robe with a shower cap on his head, holding a rather large butterfly net. "Right, here goes," Bertie said as he crept outside. "Here, little pigeon. That's right, you come here."

Bertie reached into his pocket and found an old biscuit. He had no idea how long it'd been in there, but it was perfect pigeon bait.

"That's it, come and get the stale cookie. Yummy, yummy, yummy!" Bertie whispered. He threw bits of the broken biscuit across to the pigeon as if he was a farmer throwing corn over a field. "Just a little nearer," Bertie said under his breath as the pigeon tiptoed nearer to him.

Bertie raised his fishing net and … "GOT YOU!" he said.

Perhaps *this* was his great talent. After all those years playing silly games, his actual talent was that of an expert pigeon hunter.

Bertie had seen the future and it had feathers! It almost seemed a shame that he was going to have to cook this pigeon. *How does one cook a pigeon?* Bertie thought to himself. *Perhaps the pigeon should be dead and featherless first.*

"OK, OK," Bertie said. "I can do this, but what does one do first? Does one pluck it and then kill it, or is it the other way round?"

"Excuse me, but what are you doing with my bird?"

Bertie looked round. There was a man looking over the fence at him from the next garden.

"What?!" Bertie jumped up in shock. "Who are you?" he asked. "And how long have you been standing there?"

"I'm Big Jim. Your neighbour. I've been here long enough to work out that you not only kidnapped my bird but you were going to eat her too."

"Your bird?"

"Yes, I'm a pigeon fancier," Big Jim said.

"Well, look, it's a fine-looking bird, but I don't think you're allowed to go out with pigeons, even if you do fancy them."

"No, I don't go out with pigeons. I breed them and race them." Big Jim sighed.

"You race them? How fast can they run?"

"No ... oh my, you lot haven't got a clue!" Big Jim said. "No, they race each other. I take them somewhere in my van, and then the pigeons fly home. It's a thing, it's a thing people do. They're racing pigeons, and you've just kidnapped my best flier, Bertha, and you were going to eat her. I heard you. You don't go around eating other people's pets!" Jim yelled.

"Well, I was very hungry. But I'm sorry," Bertie said. He nodded and let the bird go. "All I wanted was to do a nice thing for my family to make them like me again. I didn't think the pigeon belonged to anyone."

"Well, that's typical of you lot," Big Jim said as Bertha landed on his head. "You think you can do whatever you want!"

"What?" Bertie said.

"Listen, you lot have caused nothing but trouble since you moved in. We've had TV cameras here, someone parked an Olympic-length rowing boat on the lawn, there's been a horse nibbling on everyone's flowers."

"Erm, well ..."

"Perhaps if you thought a little bit more about other people for a change, then we'd all get along a lot better." And with that, Big Jim took Bertha and stomped off.

*

Meanwhile at St Grimley's, Harry was getting to know his new school chums, and it wasn't going well.

"Right, so this is like a school tradition, is it then?" Harry said. He was being lifted up by his underpants.

"Yeah, that's right," said a boy with spikes in his hair.

"Oh, what larks," Harry said. "I love a good tradition. We have lots in our family, although this tradition hurts a bit."

"Oh well, this is only a normal wedgie. I may have to give you the full super wedgie with a side helping of flushy too."

"What's a flushy?" Harry said, looking at the toilet, hoping it was nothing to do with that.

"It's where we stick your head in the bog and yank the chain."

"Right, well, listen here, Spike—"

"My name's not Spike, my name's Billy. It was you calling me Spike that got you into trouble in the first place."

"Well, I thought Spike would be a good nickname for you because of your hair. We used to have nicknames at my old place. There was Snotty, Kipper, Specky and Twonkers. I was just trying to make friends and fit in. I'm sorry that you and your pals Big Nose and Thicko took it the wrong way," Harry said.

"I don't think you should make fun of the way people look, and I really don't like it when someone takes my money to buy sweets ..." said Billy.

"Oh, now come on, the money had a picture of Mumsie on it. That makes it mine."

"I also don't like it when people tell me that I need to do their work for them," Billy said.

"But I always get the tutors and other boys to do my school work for me. That's how being a prince works," Harry said. Billy and his friends were still holding him up by his pants in mid-air.

"You're not a prince any more," Billy said.

"You're going to give me a flushy now, aren't you?" Harry gulped.

CHAPTER 8

Worst Day Ever

"Well, that was a joke," Betty said when she got home. "The good news is I have a bag of shopping and £235.67 in cash, but I mean, I'm so embarrassed."

She slammed the money on the table.

"I had to open a supermarket wearing a plastic crown, shouting, 'Off with these prices!' and hold up tins of beans. Then I spent an hour posing for something called selfies."

"I take it that being in showbiz isn't all that fun?" Bertie said.

"No," Betty said. "But I'm stuck with it now."

"Hey ho!" Margo said as she got home. "Great news: I'm brilliant."

"That's nice, dear." Bertie smiled.

"Brilliant at what?" Betty asked.

"Brilliant at influencing. I've been Instagramming all day and I have nearly a million followers. I've been telling everyone I meet and see in the street how to dress, speak, behave and act. I've been recording it all on the phone and posting it on the internet. I'm a hit. What's for supper?"

"Errr," Bertie said softly.

"Hmmm ... put the kettle on, Margo. I have something called a King Pot Noodle for us all. I have no idea what it is or what they put into it, but the man at Lidl said they were delicious," Betty said.

Just at that moment George walked in. He had mud all over him. "Well, that was a disaster!" He sighed. "I went to the Allotment Association, I got an allotment, I started to tend to my allotment, I even joined the committee to keep the allotments safe and tidy, when suddenly there was a big row and they threw me off."

"Why are you so dirty?" Margo asked.

"Well, there was a little problem with moles, so as part of my new job as head of pest control for the allotments, I said that I would deal with it. And ..."

"And?" Betty asked in a nervous way.

"Well, you remember Old Dickie? Well, he owed me a favour from the good old days, so I called it in, that's all," George said.

"Who's Old Dickie?" Bertie asked.

"You know, big moustache, ears like pork chops?" George explained.

"Old Dickie as in Commander Richard Nibs?" Betty asked. "Head of the Royal Air Force?"

"That's him. Anyway, he got some of his planes to carry out a bomb strike near the

cabbage patch to get rid of the moles and, well, it did a bit more damage than I'd planned."

"You bombed the allotment!" Bertie cried out.

"The moles are gone," George snapped. "You have to be ready to do what your enemy won't. It's how combat works." He shrugged.

"You bombed it?!" Betty said.

"Well, yes, a bit. Anyway, it seems that's not what the committee wanted me to do. They just wanted someone to lay the odd trap. I mean, this really is—"

"THE. WORST. DAY. EVER!" Harry said as he arrived back from his first and maybe his last

day at school. His hair was dripping wet and his undercrackers were wrapped around his head.

"What happened to you?" Betty asked.

"I had a little falling out with the boys at school. They didn't take kindly to being told what to do." Harry sighed. "Does anyone have any tweezers? I need to retrieve my underwear."

"All my followers hate me!" Margo yelled as she looked at her phone. "They're only following me because I'm 'stuck up' and make a 'complete idiot' of myself! No wonder the only bit of sponsorship I have been offered is from a kebab house and that's only because they felt sorry for me. Oh, by the way, has anyone seen Blossom? I think she's escaped again."

Betty looked around at her family, whom she loved dearly. But the truth suddenly landed on her like a ton of bricks. "People ... People don't like us, do they?" she said. It felt like she was seeing the world properly for the first time. "Because we're not very likeable. We're always telling people what to do, ordering them about," Betty said, looking at Harry and Margo. "Letting our horses run around eating people's flowers, bombing people's vegetables ..."

"Stealing their pigeons," Bertie added.

"Stealing their ... what?" Betty said.

"Nothing," Bertie added.

"No wonder people were so happy for us to fail. We've been selfish, so selfish, spending other people's money. All we do is take, take, TAKE, and do we say thank you? No, we're just used to it, we demand it, we think that we're special," Betty said.

"We *are* special – we're royals," George said.

"No, no we're not. Not any more. Look at us. We should be ashamed of the way we've treated people."

"So what are we going to do about it?" Harry asked.

"We need a plan." Betty smiled.

CHAPTER 9

Pointless Bertie

"So, what's the plan?" everyone yelled.

"What do you think we do best?" Betty cried out.

"Invade stuff?" George guessed.

"Polo?" Harry replied.

"Marrying our cousins?!" Bertie smiled.

"Lopping people's heads off?" Margo shrugged.

"Parties," said Betty. "We're good at throwing parties. We've held enough weddings, jubilees and garden parties to pick up a thing or two. One week today," she continued, "we will throw a street party, a getting-to-know-you party for the neighbours."

"Great idea. People can bring us some food and we can get a magician or someone who does something clever by bending balloons," George said, clapping his hands.

"No, we will be doing the entertaining and we will make all the food. George, you need to go back to the Allotment Association, make peace and try not to blow up any sheds. Think of this as an army exercise to win hearts and minds," Betty ordered. "Harry, why don't you invite your new school chums as a way to say sorry to them? Tell them you're sorry, and if that doesn't work, tell them there's going to be ice cream. Margo, how about giving rides on

Blossom? You might make more friends that way."

"What about me?" Bertie asked sadly.

"Bertie, I want you to ... well, if you could just ... you know, stay out of trouble."

"What are you going to do?" Bertie asked his sister.

"I'm going to spread the word. Well, I am after I go to work," Betty said, slurping back the rest of her Pot Noodle. "Yum, who knew that a Bombay Bad Boy would be so tasty?" she said, gulping the last dregs of noodle juice.

"Work?" George said.

"Yes, I have a guest spot on *Loose Women* tomorrow. We're talking about juggling jobs and families and whether us women can have it all. It's £78 in cash and as much buffet food as I can eat. After that, I'll make posters for the

party. Then I'm quitting showbiz and I'll find
something more useful to do with my time."

*

Over the next few days, the ex-royals knocked
on doors, spread the word, had chats over the
garden fence and learned their neighbours'
names. It seemed to be working: more and

more of the residents of King Street had agreed to come to the street party.

George helped the rest of the allotment guys with their harvest, and while he didn't call in any more air strikes, they were grateful to have some soldiers come in to scare away the crows.

As a reward they gave him as much fruit and veg as he wanted. They were, of course, all invited to the party.

Harry spent the rest of the week getting to know his new classmates. He even started to offer to help with their homework if they needed it, instead of expecting others to do his all the time.

Margo started to gain followers by talking about her new life and how much she was enjoying having real friends for once, not just the sort of people who want to hang around with you at parties because you're famous and loaded.

It was all going very well, the party was set for the next day and the former royals were starting to like their new life – well, most of them.

"Sis," Bertie said.

"Yes, Bertie?" Betty said, busy making curry for the party.

"I don't know what to do," he said sadly.

"What do you mean?"

"Well, everyone has a job, a purpose. Me, well, I'm just sort of knocking about the place still. I want to join in, to help, but I don't know how to. I fear I may be pointless."

"No, oh, Bertie, you have lots of uses. Remember when it was chilly the other day and we couldn't find the draft excluder, and you offered to lie down by the door so we could watch the Champions League semi-final? That was very useful. Listen, why don't you go out for a walk? You know, stay out of here? I am very busy." Betty smiled as she chopped up an onion.

"OK, sorry," Bertie said. "I will just go for a walk. Unless anyone wants me ..."

There was no reply. Everyone else in the house was busy getting ready for the street party.

"OK," Bertie said. "I'll be back, probably, soon, maybe ..." he said, walking out the front door. He looked back at the house, where everyone was busy and happy. Would they really miss him if he never came back? Perhaps it would be better if he didn't exist.

"Take another move and I'll take your head clean off." A voice came from nowhere.

"What?! Oh no!" Bertie yelled. This was it, he really was about to vanish, and no one cared a bean.

CHAPTER 10

Do the Opposite

"Please don't hurt me!" Bertie spluttered.

"Too late, punk." There was a loud ting of string and a whoosh as something flew past Bertie's head. "Oops, missed. Hang on," the voice said.

Bertie turned round to see an arrow with a sucker on one end wobbling against the fence. Bertie looked the other way and spotted a small boy holding a toy bow and arrow, trying to reload it.

"Who are you?" Bertie asked.

"I live across the street. I'm Milo."

"Oh, nice to meet you, Milo. No, no, noooo, you're doing it all wrong," Bertie said. "Let me show you. I used to have one of those when I was a kid." He grabbed the bow and arrow. "No, you put it in like this, pull it back – no, wait, hang on ..." *THWANG!* "Ow!" Bertie yelped as an arrow stuck to his head.

"Yes!" the little boy said. "That's what I was aiming for."

"No, let me try again," Bertie said, pulling the arrow off his head with a sucking sound. "Here we go, wait – OUCH!" Bertie had done the same thing again.

"You're not very good, are you?" the boy said.

"No." Bertie sighed. "In fact, I'm terrible at most things. Whatever I do, you should do the opposite," he said.

"OK, so how would you ... kick that football?" the boy asked, and pointed at one in the front garden.

"Well, I'd run really quickly at it and close my eyes and thwack it with the end of my toe."

"So, I should keep my eyes open, not rush and kick it with the side of my foot," the boy said. He gave it a go and the ball sailed perfectly through the air. "Thanks. You should be a teacher!" he said, and pulled the arrow off Bertie's head.

"That's it!" Bertie said. "You're right, I should! I know what to do with my life!"

*

The next day was the day of the street party. The tables were laid, food ready and put out, all the neighbours invited. It's strange how something as simple as having a party can make such a difference. But it did. Everyone was happy, joking, getting to know each other better and making friends. Margo was giving pony rides, Harry was entertaining the kids and George was teaching a baffled old lady how to take apart and rebuild a shotgun in under 30 seconds with a blindfold on.

Even Bertie had finally found something he was good at.

"Roll up, roll up, get your free games lessons here! Everything from Happy Families to rugby. It's simple, all you have to do is the opposite of everything I do!" Bertie said to an excited crowd of school kids.

"Who wants some of my special veggie curry?!" Betty yelled out, lifting up the ladle.

"Yes, please," an older lady said. It was Winnie from the neighbourhood watch association.

"One dollop or two?" Betty asked.

"Two, please. I skipped breakfast," Winnie said.

"Three for me, dear!" George said, charging over.

"Not with your bottom. You'll have one and like it," Betty said.

"Yes, dear," George said happily.

"How do you do it?" Winnie asked.

"Do what?" Betty asked.

"Keep everyone in check?" another lady said, coming to join the queue for curry. "Oh, I'm Jenny, by the way."

"Well, I don't know. I've been talking to prime ministers, princes and lords all my life – it's what I do. I have to keep them all in line.

Husbands and politicians are like little children. They want to get their own way, but what they really need are rules," Betty said as the crowd began to grow.

"Tell me ..." Winnie asked. "Have you ever thought about becoming a life coach? We could do with someone like you at the community centre."

*

Later on, as the street party came to a close, Betty looked around her and thought about her new life. It felt so strange that only a couple of weeks ago this place felt more like another planet than it did a home.

But what makes a place feel welcoming is not the building and how many rooms it's got or how big it is. What really makes a home is the people in it and around it.

Yes, she and her family might come from a different world from all their new friends, but they weren't so different after all. People everywhere want the same thing: somewhere safe to bring up their children, where you have friends around you, where you can have a chat

and you know that your neighbours are looking out for you.

King Street might not have been their first choice of home, but it couldn't have been a better place to end up, Betty thought to herself.

CHAPTER 11

Rock, Paper, Scissors

Several months later

"George ... George ..." Betty said, elbowing George next to her, trying to stop the loud rumble. "You're snoring again. It's Saturday, I want a lie-in."

"I thought that was you," George said, rolling over. "I ... think it's coming from outside ..."

As the room began to shake, George got up and opened the curtain. "Mmm, that's odd."

"What?" Betty asked.

"There's someone trying to land a helicopter in our garden," George said.

Betty sat up in bed and shook her head awake. She looked at George and then got up and grabbed her dressing gown. Bertie, Margo and Harry were all on the landing. They headed downstairs and out onto the street to see what all the noise was about.

A butler hopped out of the helicopter along with 17 of the country's finest trumpeters and started to yell, "Please make way for the King of England. The Lord—"

"Oh, listen, just call me King Ginger ..." Ginger said as he got out of the royal helicopter.

"Ginger?" Bertie smiled. "How are you, Your Majest—"

"Oh, please STOP!" Ginger said. "I can't take any more of it. Oh my word, it's so boring being king. All you do is visit things, see how things are made … It's like being on a really boring school trip all day every day. I can't take it any more!"

"You've only been doing it for a few months." Betty shrugged. "What did you think the job would be?"

"Well, I don't know. I thought I'd be able to go into any theme park in the world when I wanted and I wouldn't have to queue. I thought I'd have a cape made of flames, I'd get to eat ice cream for breakfast, have baths in gold coins," Ginger said. "But if I have to make any more small talk or cut another ribbon, I am going to go bananas. I want my old life back. So what do you say, Bertie, want to take me on at a little game of rock, paper, scissors? If you win, you can be royals again, and if I win, I get that … er, dressing gown," Ginger said, pointing at Bertie.

"You'd gamble it all on a dressing gown?" Betty said.

"Yes, I mean, it is a really nice one," Ginger said. "Oh, go on, you get to be queen again, you get to go home, Harry gets to go back to school, Bertie can come back to the Empire Club, Margo can do … whatever it is she does. Peeeeerlease!" Ginger begged. "Plus, I'm allergic to corgis. Go

on, Bertie, after three!" Ginger held out his fist.
"One ..."

Bertie was in a muddle. What was he to do?
I mean, he had a chance to get everything back.

"TWO!!!" Ginger yelled.

"What should I do?" he said, looking over at
Betty.

"THREE!" Ginger yelled.

Bertie closed his eyes and held out his hand.

*

Several weeks later, back at Buckingham Palace

The trumpets and bugles began to toot as
the Queen entered the kitchen.

"Yes, yes, all right. Do we really have to go
through this every time I boil the kettle?" she

yelled. "I've got a hankering for a Bombay Bad Boy."

"But we can get people to make that for you," a footman said. "Plus the Prime Minister is here to see you. Leave it with us, Your Majesty."

"Bertie, Margo, the Prime Minister's here. George, GEORGE!" the Queen yelled, heading to the living room.

"I'm here," George said.

"Sorry, this place feels so big after King Street," the Queen said as she opened the door.

"Hello, Your Majesty," said the Prime Minister, who was waiting, looking nervous. "Welcome home ..."

"Now listen here," the Queen said. "I don't want any hard feelings about everything that you said last time about us being useless. While

I wouldn't have been so blunt to *my* boss, if, well, I had one, I take your point. We were useless, spoilt, out of touch and all those mean things you said. For that I am sorry. So you can stop worrying about everything. All is forgiven," the Queen said, plonking herself down on the sofa.

"Ah, hello, Prime Minister," Bertie said, walking in with Margo.

"Well done!" the Prime Minister said to Bertie. "I hear that that little game of rock, paper, scissors is the first thing that you've ever won. Perhaps your luck is about to change." The Prime Minister smiled.

"I don't think so," Bertie said. "I put my hand out to stop Ginger and he thought it was paper. Well, he held out rock and I just sort of won. So you see, my luck's as bad as ever. I wasn't trying to win or even play, but I played and won ..." Bertie shrugged.

"It's not your fault, Bertie," Margo said. She looked quickly down at her phone, then she sighed. "I can't think of anything to vlog about. I miss my followers. Hey, Prime Minister, why don't you fire us again?!"

"I can't. The laws have been changed, so it means that none of this can happen again. I have all the documents right here," the Prime Minister said, pulling some papers out. "It says that you are royals for ever. Nothing can change that. It turns out that people thought that Ginger bloke was even worse than you were, and, well, they like the way you got stuck into life on King Street. I don't want to do the 'I told you so' thing, but I think it's fair to say that you have learned your lesson and maybe I have too – not just anyone can be a royal. Life can get back to normal."

"Your pot noodle, Your Majesty!" a butler said, bringing in a silver tray with a dish of piping noodles.

"What's this?" the Queen asked.

"Noodles, ma'am. I had our chef whip up an Indian-infused noodle broth with oriental spices."

"You call this a Pot Noodle?! I want a proper one, a Bombay Bad Boy with the bright yellow sauce in a packet. They're two for £1.50 in Lidl," the Queen yelled.

"Sorry, Your Majesty, but what's a Lidl?"

"THAT'S IT! I CAN'T TAKE ANY MORE. THAT PIECE OF PAPER SAYS I'M THE HEAD OF STATE FOR LIFE, DOES IT?" she asked the Prime Minister, who nodded.

"GOOD, THEN BY ROYAL COMMAND I DECLARE THAT WE HAVE A NEW HOME! OH, AND DON'T WORRY, I'LL RENT THIS PLACE OUT TO COVER ANY COSTS. IF ANYTHING YOU'LL BE MAKING MONEY."

"Er, OK, but this is where kings and queens live," the Prime Minister said, looking puzzled.

"I am Queen and I am going to live where I like. I can do that, can't I?" the Queen asked.

"Well, yes, I suppose, but where do you want to go? You have everything here!" the Prime Minister said.

"No, I don't," the Queen yelled.

"I don't have my allotment," George said.

"I don't have anything to make videos about," Margo yelled.

"I don't have my games class," Bertie said.

"And I don't have Winnie or Jenny or the chance to talk to people, say hello, gossip over the fence or go to a Lidl round the corner. I am queen and my public need me, but not as much as I need them." The Queen smiled. "I want to go back to King Street. This palace may be where queens and kings have always lived, but this isn't our home."